This igloo book belongs to:

....ORLA GH........CHRISTMAS 2014....

Published in 2014
by Igloo Books Ltd
Cottage Farm
Sywell
NN6 0BJ
www.igloobooks.com

SHE001 0714
4 6 8 10 9 7 5
ISBN: 978-1-78197-528-2

Printed and manufactured in China

Illustrated by Susie Poole, Paul and Alice Sharp,
Shelagh McNicholas and Michelle Todd and Mike Garton.

My First Stories for Girls

igloobooks

Contents

Stories for 1 Year Old Girls

Molly's Pretty Picture

Molly gets out her paints that are red, yellow and blue.
She has a pretty apron and lots of crayons, too.

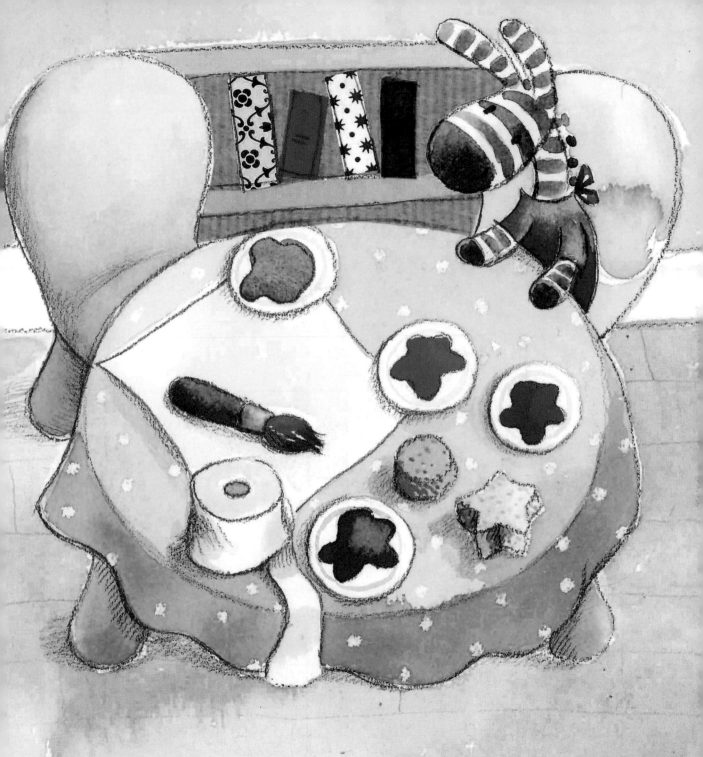

She is making a picture for Mommy to see.
Molly says, "It's a present for Mommy, from me!"

9

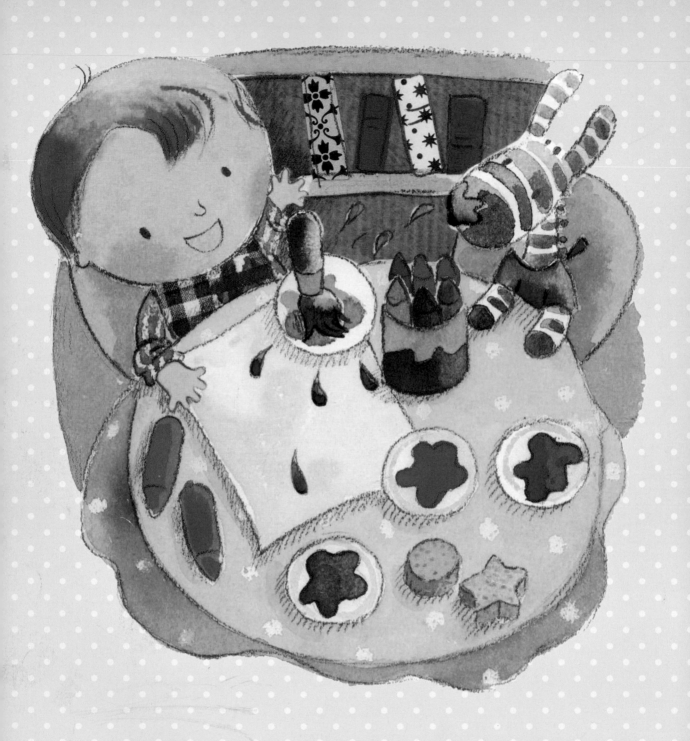

Molly drops her brush into the paint with a plop.
She splats it about with a splodge and a slop.

On a piece of paper, Molly draws funny wiggles.
She paints all over it with long, swirly squiggles!

11

Then, Molly puts her hands in the paint with a splat.
She makes patterns on the page with a big, squishy pat.

To finish the picture, Molly adds some swirls fast.
Then, she gives Mommy her present at last.

Mommy reaches up high, because she is very tall.
She sticks Molly's pretty picture up onto the wall.

14

Molly has a bubble bath, then it is time for a rest.
"Thank you, Molly," says Mommy.
"My picture is the best!"

Woofy Puppy

Woofy Puppy is Bella's best friend.
They do everything together.

Woofy Puppy wakes Bella up every
morning and licks her on the nose.
Bella loves to give her puppy a big cuddle.

Woofy Puppy follows Bella everywhere.
When she runs away, Woofy Puppy chases her.

"Let's hide in our cushion den," says Bella.
"Woof," agrees Woofy Puppy.

Woofy Puppy and Bella play fun games, like
hide-and-seek, in the garden.

When Bella goes down the slide,
Woofy Puppy slides down, too!

When she has a bath, Bella makes
Yellow Duck squeak and Woofy Puppy barks.

At bedtime, Bella gives Woofy Puppy a hug.
"I love you, Woofy Puppy," she says.

Rainbow Room

My rainbow room is a great place to play.
There are lots of fun things here to look at today.

Some toys are hidden in my blue toy chest.
The things kept inside it are always the best.

25

Ring-ring, goes the telephone. It is shiny and red.
It jiggles and rattles right next to my bed.

I love to hug Teddy. He is furry and purpley-blue.
He gives big, squashy cuddles to my daddy, too.

Boing-boing! I love to play with my pink, bouncy ball.
It **thumps** off the floor and the door and the wall.

28

My little green car goes **vroom-vroom-vroom**.
It drives across the floor with a **zip-zip-zoom**.

The best things to play with, of all my toys,
are the ones that make lots of music and noise.

My piano **tinkle-tinkles** when I play a song
and my big, noisy drum goes, **bang-bang-bong!**

31

Izzy in the Car

Izzy has been to the shop with Daddy.
Now it is time to drive all the way back home.

The car goes **vroom-vroom** down the road.
Izzy can see lots of things through the window.

Daddy drives past the play park.
Izzy can see children on the swings,
going **swoosh**-**swoosh** up into the air.

Izzy sees three little ducklings, going **quack-quack**! They are **splish-splashing** with their Mommy in the pond.

35

Izzy can see lots of people sitting on the big, red bus.
The bus driver sounds her loud horn, **beep-beep**!

She waves to the postman on his shiny bicycle.
He waves back and rings his noisy bell, **ding-ding**!

When Daddy and Izzy get home,
Mommy is waiting on the doorstep.
"Hello," says Mommy. She gives Izzy a big hug.

Izzy loves going out for a drive in the car with Daddy,
but best of all, she likes coming home.

39

The Red Raincoat

Daisy loves her raincoat. It is red and very bright.
It has round, blue buttons all down the front.

When Daddy and Daisy are at the park,
Daddy does the buttons up one by one.

When Daisy goes on the slide, her fingers get very cold.
She opens her big pocket. **Swish** goes the zipper.

Daisy pulls out a pair of woolly, warm mittens.
Daddy helps Daisy to put them on, nice and snug.

When it starts to rain, with big plip-plops of water,
Daisy's hood keeps her head nice and dry.

Daisy wears shiny boots to keep her feet dry, too.
She loves to jump in puddles, going **splish** and **splash**.

45

Daisy's raincoat has kept her nice and warm and dry.
She is sad to take it off when she gets inside.

Daisy loves her raincoat. She loves the
blue buttons, big pockets and cosy hood.
"I hope it rains again soon," says Daisy.

47

My Best Dolly

I love my dolly. She has long hair and pretty, green eyes. She wears a beautiful dress with big, purple flowers.

Me and my dolly always play at dressing-up.
I like to make her look like a pretty princess.

My dolly loves to sit with Mommy and me at storytime.
We look at the pictures together.

Dolly stays with me when I clean my teeth.
Mommy brushes my hair and I brush my dolly's hair, too.

My dolly is lovely to go to sleep with at bedtime.
She is always with me and she is the best dolly, ever!

Stories for 2 Year Old Girls

Lily's Lovely Garden

Lily is in her lovely garden. It is time to play outside.
She loves the leafy trees and her super-slippy slide.

Mommy pushes Lily's swing and she **swooshes** up so high.
Lily wants to touch the clouds and swish across the sky.

Mommy plants some pretty flowers in a neat and tidy row.
Lily helps to plant them, too. She can't wait for them to grow.

Lily pours on lots of water to give the flowers a drink.
They will grow up big and strong and be really bright and pink.

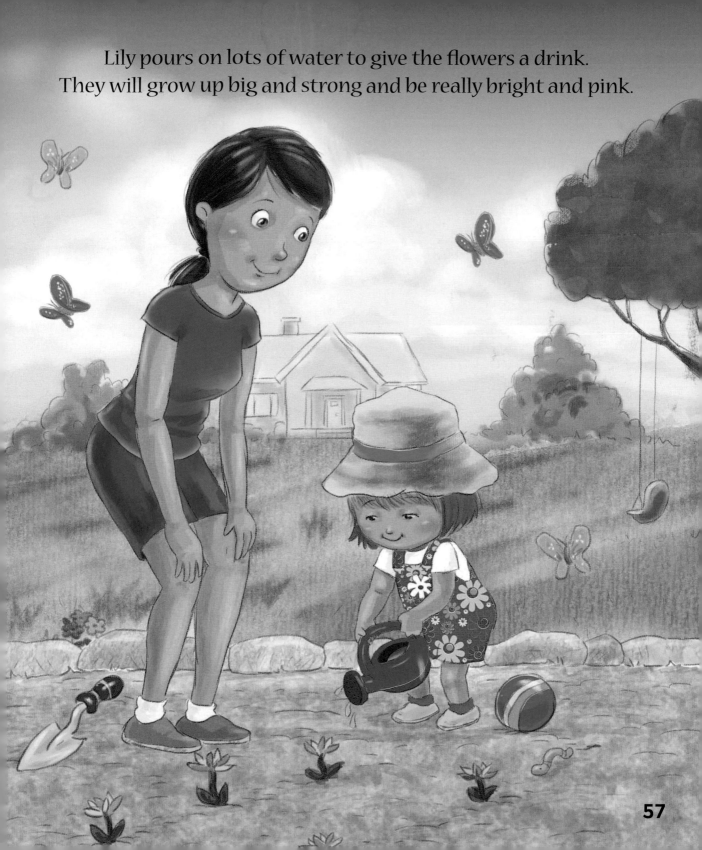

When Lily has finished watering, she runs off to explore.
She finds all sorts of insects, like spiders, ants and more.

"Hello," says Lily, when she finds a dotty ladybug.
It is sitting on a leaf, looking happy, warm and snug.

Lily plays outside until it's nearly the end of the day.
She runs to tell her mother that the sun has gone away.

60

Mommy wraps Lily in a blanket and she curls up for a rest.
She can't wait to play outside again. Her garden is the best.

61

Rosie's Bedtime

Rosie is getting sleepy. She has had lots of fun today.
It is time to get ready to go to bed and put her toys away.

"Come on, Rosie," Mommy says. "Your bubble bath is ready.
We can play with Yellow Duck and put pajamas on, like Teddy."

63

In the tub with Yellow Duck, Rosie has a soapy wash.
She pops the bubbles and splashes water with a giant **splosh**.

Mommy sits on the edge of the tub, next to Rosie's bear.
She dries Rosie with a towel and combs her curly hair.

Wrapped up in a towel, Rosie thinks she looks very funny.
Mommy says, "Here are your pajamas with a picture of a bunny."

Rosie wiggles into her pajamas and pulls the top over her head.
She grabs Teddy's little paw and jumps into her cosy bed.

Mommy reads a bedtime story from her special book.
Rosie loves the pictures. She makes sure Teddy has a look.

When Rosie is sleepy, Mommy kisses and hugs her tight.
"I love you lots, Mommy," says Rosie. "Night, night."

Cleo the Kitten

Cleo is my little, black and white kitten. She is very bouncy and very cute. She loves to run around and pounce on wiggly bits of string.

I follow Cleo when she explores the garden. She leaps between the flower bushes. She runs round and round, chasing spiders and little butterflies.

Sometimes, Cleo is a very naughty, little kitten.
Mommy does not like it when Cleo climbs up the drapes.

Cleo is very good at hiding. Sometimes I can't find her anywhere, but she always comes back if I get her a tasty treat.

When I am painting pictures with my brushes and paint, Cleo likes to run across them and leave paw prints all over the floor.

Cleo knocks things over when she runs past tables and chairs,
but she is so cute that she gets away with everything.

Cleo loves it when I pour her a big saucer of milk.
She laps it all up, but she always wants more.

When I stroke Cleo's back, or rub her ears, she purrs and purrs.
I love Cleo very much. She really is the best kitten ever.

Clara's Cake

Mommy is making a special cake for someone.
"It will be a lovely surprise for them," says Mommy.
"Please can I help?" asks Clara.

"Yes," replies Mommy. She helps Clara put on a pretty, flowery apron. Then, she washes Clara's hands with warm, soapy water.

Mommy measures out all the ingredients that they will need. Clara helps to tip everything into a big, pink mixing bowl.

"Now we need to mix everything together," says Mommy.
Clara stirs the mixture as fast as she can.
Then, Mommy pours it into a tin.

81

When the cake is in the oven, Clara and Mommy
make some pink and purple frosting.
The frosting is very sticky, but it tastes lovely!

Mommy takes the cake out of the oven
and lets Clara spread the frosting on.
Clara puts extra-tasty toppings all over it, too.

Mommy cuts two slices and makes a drink.
"Can you guess who the cake is for?" she asks.
"No," replies Clara.

"It's for me and you," says Mommy and Clara giggles. Then, she and Mommy have a big slice each of their best ever cake.

Hattie's Bath Time

Hattie loves getting messy. At breakfast, she splodges porridge and milk down her clean t-shirt. She gets jam all over her face.

Mommy says, "You look like you need a bath."
"No!" says Hattie, running out into the garden.
She thinks bath time is boring.

Hattie loves to play outside. In the garden, she can get really mucky. She squelches through the mud and crawls under leafy hedges.

When Hattie comes inside, she has mud splattered all over her face and her top. She even has twigs in her hair. Mommy says, "Now you really need a bath!"

"No!" says Hattie. She still does not want to have a bath.
She wants to go back outside and play with
the creepy-crawlies.

Mommy says she has a special surprise for Hattie.
"This is Mr Whale. You can play with him in
the tub," says Mommy.

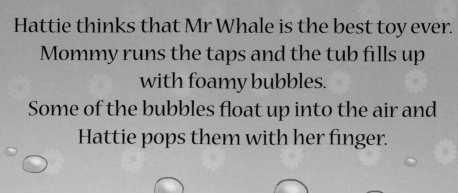

Hattie thinks that Mr Whale is the best toy ever.
Mommy runs the taps and the tub fills up
with foamy bubbles.
Some of the bubbles float up into the air and
Hattie pops them with her finger.

92

Hattie gets in the bath. She has lots of fun
playing with Mr Whale and Mommy, too.
"I love bath time!" says Hattie.

My Big Sister

I love my big sister because she is so much fun.
She pulls funny faces and tells silly jokes.

My sister likes to draw pretty flowers and butterflies. Sometimes I draw a squiggly picture for her and she says it is really good.

95

When my sister gets dressed up in a pretty dress, I do too.
She loves to wear lots of pink and gold and so do I!

My sister shows me how to put my hair
up in pretty plaits, just like hers.
She puts flowers in my hair so that our hairstyles match.

I love my big sister because she gives soft, snuggly cuddles.
She loves to hug me tight. She is the best sister ever.

Stories for

3

Year Old Girls

The Sparkly Shoes

Fairy Twinkle was trying out her new wand. She wanted a pair of sparkly shoes, just like her friend, Cherrybud. **Zing!**
She swished her wand, but a pair of old, blue boots appeared.

Twinkle tried again. This time, she waved her wand a
bit harder. There was a cloud of sparkles. When Twinkle
looked down, she was wearing a pair of funny,
yellow flippers.

"I must be doing it wrong," said Twinkle. "Maybe I need some magic words." She thought very hard and then said, "I want lovely shoes that shine. Bring me shoes that are all mine."

Suddenly, a pair of orange shoes appeared, then a blue
pair, then a white pair and a purple pair, too. More shoes
appeared every minute. "Help!" cried Twinkle. "Make them stop!"

Cherrybud came to help. She waved her wand and all of the shoes disappeared. "You just need to say the right words," said Cherrybud.

"Bring to Twinkle shoes that shimmer.
One red pair that glitter and glimmer."

Twinkle said the magic words and a pair of sparkly, red shoes appeared. "Thank you, Cherrybud," she said, with a big smile. The two fairies played happily in their sparkly shoes and Twinkle was so pleased to have such a wonderful best friend.

Flora at the Fair

Flora had never been to the Fairy Funfair before. She wasn't sure that she liked the loud music, or the flashing lights. **Whoosh!** went a big, twirly ride that span round and round.

Everything seemed so big and there were lots of loud noises.
"I'm scared," said Flora. She held on to her mother's hand tightly.
"Don't worry," said Mom. "The fair is lots of fun."

Mom bought Flora an enormous stick of delicious, pink, sticky cotton candy. "It's yummy," said Flora. All around them, big rides **whizzed** and **whooshed**. Then, Flora spotted a little, blue train. "I want to go on that," she said.

The blue train chugged, as it went up and down the curvy track. "This isn't scary at all!" said Flora. **Toot, toot!** went the little, blue train. Flora thought that maybe the fair wasn't so bad after all.

109

Next, Flora played the hook-a-duck game. She stretched
as far as she could and suddenly, she hooked a
yellow duck with the number 1 on it.
"You've won a giant teddy!" cried Mom. "Well done, Flora."

Flora took her giant teddy on the teacup ride. She giggled happily as they swirled and whirled round and round. "I'm not scared anymore," said Flora. "I think being at the fair is lots of fun."

Dancing Charlotte

Princess Charlotte loved to dance, but it was no fun on her own. "Please dance with me," she begged her dad. So, the king tried to waltz with Charlotte, but he kept treading on her toes.

"I'll dance with you," said the queen. "I used to love twirling at the annual royal ball!" She took Charlotte's hands and whirled her round and round, until the queen started to feel very dizzy.

Charlotte tried some ballet with the butler and tap-danced
with the royal cook. She twirled and whirled with
everyone in the palace and soon they had to sit down,
because they were all exhausted!

"I want to keep dancing," said Charlotte, but everyone was too tired. Charlotte was very disappointed. "What you need is a party," said the queen, "with lots of music and dancing."

So, the king and queen invited all of Princess Charlotte's
friends to a royal music party. The music started and
everyone bopped, bounced and boogied to the beat.
It was so much fun.

Charlotte loved her special music party. "Thank you, Mom and Dad,"
she said. "Dancing with grown-ups in the palace was fun,
but dancing with all of my best friends is much better!"

The Scary Storm

Sparkle was picking daisies in the meadow when suddenly, a huge, dark storm cloud appeared. "Oh, no," squeaked Sparkle, feeling scared. Just then, a flash of lightning streaked across the sky.

The frightened fairy flitted into the woods to hide. She flew as fast as she could, as thunder boomed and rumbled above the treetops. Soon, Sparkle's wings were worn out and she had to stop to rest.

Plop! A raindrop landed on Sparkle's head. "I'm scared and I'm lost," she said, sadly. "Now I'm getting all wet, too." Sparkle was about to cry when she saw two little fairies carrying purple petal umbrellas.

"Hello. We're Splish and Splash, the storm fairies," they said.
"Don't be frightened. Storms are lots of fun."
Splish and Splash showed Sparkle how to jump
between puddles and how to dance so that the
water splashed everywhere.

121

Splish turned her petal umbrella upside down and the three friends climbed inside. They spent all afternoon bobbing along the Rainbow River. Soon, the sun was shining brightly again. "It's time for us to go," said the storm fairies.

Sparkle's new friends took her back to the meadow and
waved goodbye as they fluttered away. "I'll look out
for you next time it thunders," said Sparkle.
"I'll never be scared of storms again."

The Pink Party

Princess Rosy loved pink. She wore pink clothes, ate pink candy and even had a pretty pink poodle as a pet. So, on her birthday, Rosy really wanted everything at her party to be pink.

The queen gave Rosy a bright orange and red dress to wear to the party. "Thank you," said the princess. She thought the dress was very pretty, but there was just one problem. It wasn't pink!

Then, the royal cook came in carrying a giant
green and yellow birthday cake. Rosy thought it
looked lovely and very yummy, but it still wasn't pink,
so she was very disappointed.

When her friends arrived, Rosy thanked them for the
presents that they gave her, even though none of them
were pink. The queen saw that the princess was sad
and suddenly realised what was wrong.

The queen asked the cook to whip up some pink cupcakes.
Then, she quickly put up lots and lots of pink decorations.
Finally, she found some pink ribbons and tied
them into bows to add to Rosy's dress.

"I thought you might want a change from pink," said
the queen. "Now I can see that you like it more than ever!"
Rosy gave her mom a giant hug.
Her party was perfectly pink after all.

The Magical Unicorn

My unicorn is the best. Together, we fly high above the sparkly, cotton-candy clouds. We say hello to the little birds that we see, as we **whoosh** past the glittery rainbows in the Fairyland sky.

We stop at the Lemonade River for a yummy picnic with
my best fairy friends. There are caramel cupcakes
and strawberry pastries for everybody to eat.
My unicorn sometimes gets a treat, too!

Sometimes, we fly to the Lollipop Wood. We jump and twirl around the lollipop trees, while our unicorns munch on the tasty grass. My unicorn is always friendly and kind to everyone.

When the bright moon and stars appear in the sky, my unicorn flies me home. "Goodnight," I say to my unicorn, giving him a hug. "Thank you for being the best unicorn ever."

The Best Friend Necklace

Princess Zara and Princess Anna were best friends.
One day, when they were playing dressing-up, Zara found
a beautiful necklace. "This will go perfectly with my purple
shoes," said Anna, snatching it from Zara's hand.

"It would look better with my orange ones," said Zara, crossly pulling the necklace back. The princesses tugged it back and forth between them, until suddenly, the lovely necklace **snapped** in half.

Just then, Anna's mom called, saying it was time for
Anna to go home. Zara sadly watched her best friend
leave, still holding one half of the necklace.
She had never fought with Anna before.

136

The queen saw how sad Princess Zara was and asked her what had happened. Zara told the queen all about the broken necklace. "I've got an idea," said the queen. "What if you made Princess Anna a special present?"

The next day, Princess Zara and the queen went to visit Princess Anna. "I'm sorry for fighting with you," said Zara. She handed Anna a new heart necklace, made from half of the necklace they had snapped in two.

"I made you a present, too," giggled Anna. She gave Zara a necklace made from the other broken half! It had a shiny star pendant on it. The two princesses hugged. They knew they were going to be best friends forever.

The Painting Princesses

It was a rainy day, so Princess Amelia and Princess Harriet got out their paintbrushes and paint pots. "Let's paint a picture of daddy," they said. "Try not to make a mess," said the queen.

Amelia sploshed her paintbrush in the pink pot and drew a small circle. Harriet splished her brush in the purple pot and drew a big circle. **Splish**, **splash**, they went, as they splodged bright paint all over the page.

Splodge, **splat**! Harriet painted a red nose. "I will paint him some arms and legs, " said Amelia. She stuck her fingers in a pot of orange paint and splatted it onto the paper.

The princesses splatted and splashed until they were
covered in paint. Just then, the king came in. "What an
interesting picture you've painted," he said.
"Is it a monster?"

Princess Harriet and Princess Amelia both giggled.
"It's a picture of you, Daddy," they said.
"It can go in the royal gallery," said the king, laughing,
"but first, you two had better have a bath!"

144

Stories for

4

Year Old Girls

Princess Maisy's Music Lesson

It was time for Princess Maisy's piano lesson. "Oh no!" said the queen. The king put his earplugs in and the royal dog ran into the garden to hide. The princess was not very good at playing the piano!

No matter how hard Maisy tried, the music she played always sounded terrible. Her teacher, Mr Melody, covered his ears when Maisy plinked and plonked loudly on the piano keys. "Maybe you should try a different instrument," he suggested.

At lunch, Princess Maisy clanged her fork on her plate and tapped on the table with her fingers. The queen had a headache after hearing Maisy play the piano. "Why don't you help the royal cook bake a cake, Maisy?" she said.

In the kitchen, Princess Maisy helped Cook to get out all the trays and pans. She banged and crashed everything down onto the table. Mr Melody was walking past and heard the crashing and banging. "Hmmm," he said, "that gives me an idea."

At Princess Maisy's next lesson, there was a big surprise.
"We've bought you a drum kit!" cried the king. Maisy picked up
the pink drumsticks and played a noisy beat. "I think Maisy is
going to be very good on the drums," said Mr Melody.

"Music lessons are going to be so much fun!" Maisy giggled, hitting the cymbals with a huge crash. The king and queen smiled. Maisy was going to be as noisy as ever, but she was very happy and besides, they always had their earplugs.

The Fairy Gown

Lunabell and Silverwing were very excited when they got an invitation to the Fairy Queen's birthday party. "We've got to be the best-dressed fairies there," said Lunabell. "Come on, let's go to Miss Cherrybead's Fairy Fashion Shop."

The two fairies quickly flitted off to the shop,
but ahead of them they saw lots of other fairies flying in
the same direction. "Hurry up!" cried Silverwing. "It looks like
everyone in Sparkle Wood has had the same idea as us."

153

There was a long queue of fairies outside the shop. Finally, Lunabell and Silverwing reached the front, but when they stepped inside, they saw that the shop was almost empty. Miss Cherrybead looked tired. "I'm sorry," she said, "but there's only one dress left."

"It's mine!" cried Lunabell, grabbing the top of the dress.
"No, I want it!" shouted Silverwing, grabbing the bottom.
The two fairies pulled and tugged. Suddenly, the dress ripped
in half. "Sparkle Wood is supposed to be a happy place!" cried
Miss Cherrybead. "If fairies argue, the magic disappears."

Silverwing and Lunabell ran outside. All around the fashion shop, the magic was fading from Sparkle Wood. The clouds became very dark and it began to rain. "Oh no," said Lunabell. "We've got to get the magic back before the Fairy Queen's birthday party."

The two fairies had an idea. They asked Miss Cherrybead
if they could take one half of the dress each.
Silverwing used her half to make a beautiful new dress
for Lunabell and Lunabell did the same for Silverwing.

157

Once Silverwing and Lunabell had put on their lovely new dresses, all the magic came flooding back to Sparkle Wood. The two friends hugged. "We did it!" cried Lunabell.

"Let's never fall out again," said Silverwing, with a big smile.

At the Fairy Queen's party, Silverwing and Lunabell ate delicious cupcakes and danced all night long. Everyone loved their dresses. The two fairies were glad that Sparkle Wood was magical again, but they were even more pleased to be friends.

The Mysterious Maze

Princess Freya was moving into a beautiful, new palace, but she wasn't very happy. "I liked our old castle better," said Freya to the queen, as she carried a box of toys inside. "I don't have any friends to play with here."

"Why don't you explore the palace?" said the queen. "You might find something fun to do." So, Freya went exploring and soon, she discovered a secret attic room. She opened an old chest and it was full of beautiful ball gowns.

161

"I wish my friends were here to play dress-up with,"
sighed Freya. She tried a blue gown on and twirled by
the window. Then, Freya spotted a maze in the palace garden.
"Wow!" she cried, running downstairs to get a better look.

162

When Freya walked into the maze, she could hear a funny giggling noise coming from the other side of the hedges. She followed the twists and turns for a long time, until suddenly, she came across two other princesses.

"Hi," said one princess. "Have you just moved in next door? We hope you don't mind us playing in your maze."

"Of course not," said Freya, happily. "I'm Freya. Do you want to come and play dress-up with me sometime?"

The princesses said yes straight away, so Freya led them back to her palace. She showed them the chest full of pretty gowns and they played together all afternoon. Freya realised that moving palace might be really fun after all.

165

The Fastest Fairy

One sunny day, the fairies decided to have a flying race.
They all wanted to win first prize. Lilybell was the
smallest fairy and she could not fly as fast as the others.
She looked sadly at her tiny wings.

"If I come last, the big fairies will laugh at me,"
Lilybell sadly told her best friend, Honeycup.
"You just need a bit of practice, silly," said Honeycup.
Lilybell thought this was a good idea. She set off
to start straight away.

167

The little fairy concentrated as hard as she could. She bent her knees and launched herself into the air. Lilybell soared upwards, but suddenly, her hair blew into her eyes and she flew, with a thump, right into the middle of a giant flower.

The older fairies giggled and pointed at Lilybell.
Although she was very embarrassed, Lilybell was so
determined to keep practicing that she got up and tried again.
Jumping from the giant flower's pink petals, Lilybell
zoomed away at super-fast speed.

169

Splat! Suddenly, Lilybell was caught in a sticky spiderweb. She had been flying so fast, she hadn't seen the silvery strands. She quickly untangled herself, but behind her, Lilybell could hear the big fairies laughing very loudly.

Feeling really cross, Lilybell stomped off to practise on her own.
She found the perfect spot and began to flutter her wings
as fast as she could. Whizzing and whooshing, Lilybell flew
between the trees, straight into a prickly bramble bush.

By the time Lilybell had climbed out of the prickly bush, the race was about to start. She quickly lined up alongside the big fairies. "Watch out for flowers and spiderwebs," said one and the big fairies all giggled.

Lilybell felt so angry that she blasted away the moment the
race began. She whizzed past the bigger fairies and swooshed
over the finish line first, to whoops and cheers from the crowd.
From then on, everyone agreed that Lilybell was
the fastest fairy by far.

173

Poppy's Pet

In Fairyland, Poppy's friends were playing with their pets. Sasha cuddled her cute, fluffy bunny and Fizz stroked her little, white mouse. They looked like they were having fun. "I wish I had a pet, too," said Poppy, sadly.

Just then, Poppy noticed something wiggling on
the ground. It was a cute little caterpillar. Poppy held
out her hand and the caterpillar wriggled onto it.
"You're very tickly," said Poppy. "I think you
will make a perfect pet."

Poppy loved her caterpillar. He may have been very small,
but he had a huge appetite. He ate and ate all day long.
He chomped through leaves and munched on fruit.
Poppy's caterpillar just couldn't get enough to eat.

Then, one day, someone nibbled all of the Fairy Queen's magic flowers. "It must have been your caterpillar, Poppy," said Sasha and Fizz. "He's going to be in trouble," said Poppy. "I have to find him." Poppy searched everywhere, but her caterpillar had disappeared.

"The Fairy Queen will be so cross and my caterpillar has gone,"
sobbed Poppy. "I'm not cross," said a soft voice. It was the
Fairy Queen. She showed Poppy where her caterpillar was
hiding, fast asleep. "When he wakes, he will look
quite different," she said.

178

Poppy waited and watched. One morning, as if by magic,
she saw that her caterpillar had turned into a beautiful butterfly.
"It must have been those magic flowers!" she cried.
Poppy was very happy. Now she really did have the best pet ever.

Wanda's Sparkly Wings

It was the Fairy Queen's birthday and Wanda had made her some lovely birthday cupcakes. There was going to be a big party. Wanda wanted her wings to look extra sparkly, so she covered them in all sorts of pretty beads and sequins.

When Wanda was ready, she grabbed the cupcakes and zoomed outside. As Wanda fluttered along, her wings drooped. The sparkly decorations had made them too heavy to fly with! Suddenly, Wanda fell on top of the cupcakes, with a big splat.

181

"Oh no!" sobbed Wanda. Just then, her friends Evie and Clara came around the corner. They helped Wanda take the heavy beads and sequins off her wings. Suddenly, Wanda realised that she had nothing to give the Fairy Queen for her birthday.

"Don't worry," said Clara. "We can make something else for the queen," The fairies gathered the shiny beads and sequins from Wanda's wings, then found some strands of fairy silk and twisted them all together. "Perfect," said Evie. "Let's go to the party."

At the party, Wanda, Evie and Clara gave the Fairy Queen
her present. It was a necklace made of all the sparkly decorations
from Wanda's wings. The Fairy Queen smiled as Wanda told her
what had happened on the way to the party.

"Never mind, there's plenty of birthday cake to go around already," said the Fairy Queen. "Thank you for my beautiful necklace." She waved her wand and the three fairies' wings all sparkled brightly. "You shall be the three sparkliest fairies at the party after all."

Princess Belle's Bedtime

It was Princess Belle's bedtime, but she felt wide awake. She didn't want to go to sleep yet. "Princesses can't go to sleep without their teddy bears," said Belle, when the king came to tuck her in, "and I can't find mine anywhere."

The king laughed as Belle bounced up and down on the bed. "Well, I've just found him in the washing machine," said the king, holding Teddy up. "I wonder how he could have got there? Now, it's really time for you to go to bed, Belle."

Belle shook her head and said, "A princess can't go to bed until she's had some cookies and milk." With a big sigh, the king took Belle to the palace kitchen and found her some cookies. "When you've finished those, it's really time for bed," said the king.

Princess Belle giggled. "I still can't go to bed yet," she said, "because I haven't brushed my teeth, Daddy. Princesses have got to have nice, white smiles." The king gave Belle a funny frown and tapped his foot, while Belle brushed and brushed.

There was one more thing that Belle thought a princess needed before going to sleep. "Can you read me a bedtime story, Daddy?" she asked. The king read Belle a magical fairytale, but almost as soon as he started reading, Princess Belle finally fell fast asleep.

Activity Page

See if you can answer these questions about the stories in 'My First Pretty Stories For Girls'.

1. Where do Bella and Woofy Puppy hide in 'Woofy Puppy'?

2. Who does Clara make her cake with in 'Clara's Cake'?

3. Who helps Sparkle stay safe in 'The Scary Storm'?

4. Which instrument is Princess Maisy really good at playing in 'Princess Maisy's Music Lesson'?

All of these characters are featured in this book. Can you find them and write down the page that they are on?

Answers: 1. Cushion Den 2. Clara's Mommy 3. Splish and Splash, the storm fairies. 4. The drums. 5. Page 17, 6. Page 73, 7. Page 123, 8. Page 159

"Goodbye and see you soon!"